The Wolves of Glastonbury

By Terrie Leigh Relf
& Edward Cox

The Wolves of Glastonbury
By Terrie Leigh Relf & Edward Cox

All rights reserved. No part of this book may be reproduced or transmitted in any form or by any means, electronic or mechanical, including photocopying or recording or by any information storage and retrieval systems, without expressed written consent of the author and/or artists.

The Wolves of Glastonbury is a work of fiction. Names, characters, places, and incidents are products of the author's imagination. Any resemblance to actual events or persons, living or dead, is entirely coincidental.

Story copyright owned by Terrie Leigh Relf and Edward Cox

Cover illustration "Glastonbury" © 2016 by Teresa Tunaley

Cover design by Laura Givens

First Printing, April 2016
Second Printing, November 2024

Hiraeth Publishing
P.O. Box 1248
Tularosa, NM 88352
e-mail: tyreealban@gmail.com

Visit www.albanlake.com for science fiction, fantasy, dark fiction, and more. Support the small, independent press...

Also by Edward Cox:

Published by Gollancz:
The Relic Guild
The Cathedral of Known Things

Also by Terrie Leigh Relf:

Published by Hiraeth Publishing:
The Poet's Workshop and Beyond
Sisterhood of the Blood Moon
An Untoward Bliss of Moons
The Waters of Nyr

Blood Journey [with Henry Lewis Sanders]
The Ancient One [with Sanders]

The Wolves of Glastonbury

-RUSTIC SILVER-

Ethan was dying.

Naked and alone, his skin glistening with sweat and blood, he stumbled through the darkness, wading through tall stalks of corn that whipped at his skin. He pressed a hand against the bullet wound in his side, and blood oozed from between his fingers. With a quick and desperate glance behind him, he saw the lights of a farmhouse winking in the distance, but no sign of the shadows hunting him. A solitary sob of relief escaping his lips, Ethan headed towards the silhouette of an old disused barn on the far side of the cornfield, hoping that it would at least make a peaceful haven in which he could await the end.

The aged doors complained as they swung outwards, juddering on little-used hinges. Falling inside the barn, he smelt rotten wood and hot dirt. All around sprawled the rusted skeletons of outmoded machinery and tools. Part of the roof had collapsed, exposing the bright silver moon and stars above.

Crawling to a set of creaky steps, Ethan dragged himself up into an empty hayloft. He lay down on his back upon the bare boards, and they groaned under his weight. Breathing hard, he stared through the hole in the roof, and up at the twinkling night sky. The summer air was hot, filled with musty scents and the clicks of crickets. Here, in this place, it felt as though there were no longer any mobile phones, TVs and computers; no aeroplanes, cars or global warming - just a simpler existence, a return to a time where mod cons were not life's dominant force, a place where he liked being.

He could smell the blood that ran from his side and soaked into the wood beneath him. It was an earthy scent, wholesome, somehow apt. The wound didn't hurt so much now that he lay still. As far as he could tell, the bullet had missed any organ or bone, and had passed clean through him, but the silver it was made from had poisoned his blood. He could feel its corrosion spreading through his veins.

Ethan wondered if his death was for the best. When his body was found, they would say he was just a dead lunatic, the village idiot who got what he deserved at the hands of vigilantes serving their own brand of parochial justice. How many would weep for his passing?

But he wouldn't trade anything or change one aspect of events that led to this moment. Strange that at the brink of death he should discover how life could expand with such freedom, such acceptance. Better to have felt that for a single moment than live an entire life in ignorance. No. Ethan wouldn't change a single thing.

Down below, the barn doors creaked open, and Ethan's breath caught in his throat. Perhaps they had tracked him. Perhaps they had come with pitchfork and torch, like the stories of old. Perhaps they would simply burn the barn to the ground and spread his ashes into myth and fable.

A moment passed, and Ethan relaxed as he heard the gentle panting of hot breath, smelt the musky odour of a damp pelt. A sad smile touched his lips. He should have known she would come back, to be here with him at the end.

You fool, he thought. *You should've run – and kept running - while you had the chance . . .*

And with this thought, Ethan found his one and only regret, the one thing that he would change: how they had waited so long to be together . . .

-I-
The Chimp

Books. Too many to read in one lifetime, and that was a source of sadness to Ethan. He took consolation from their existence, however, and felt comforted that working at Glover's Bookshop kept him surrounded by stories, by history, by knowledge.

It was Monday morning, and Ethan was hidden away, correcting the alphabetical order of the titles in the philosophy aisle. The weekend browsers had grabbed, flicked, and then discarded, caring nothing that Nietzsche came after Kierkegaard, that Aristotle and Confucius didn't mix well. In truth, Ethan enjoyed the chance to handle these tomes, reorganising and showing them proper respect. Today, he was alone in the shop; his boss, Mark, hadn't materialised yet, and very often didn't at the beginning of the week, leaving Ethan to open and close all by himself. He enjoyed the solitude.

People barely acknowledged Ethan's existence anyway, and he preferred it that way. They rarely asked questions, and when they did, they never waited for an answer. Like a ghost drifting on the periphery, Ethan and his life outside Glover's Bookshop was unimportant to all, and it was safer if it remained so.

As the morning wore on, he moved from aisle to aisle, section to section, re-sorting the order of authors dead and alive, and he was as happy in his work as he was in his own company. But it was while he sorted the horror section that Ethan's peaceful world was shattered. He could hear Mark speaking even before he entered the shop. At the best of times, Ethan's boss was too loud, too sure of himself. Brash. Yes, Mark was brash - pompous as well – and that was being polite.

Ethan's shoulders sagged as the shop door tinkled open. He kept himself hidden in the horror aisle as Mark entered while in mid-conversation with someone.

". . . Of course," he was saying, "this shop is just a

hobby really, something to keep me busy. The real money is in father's farms. But I don't mind telling you, I've never particularly enjoyed the smell of manure." He laughed. He always laughed at his own jokes.

"I'm used to the smell," came a polite reply. "There were a lot of farms where I grew up." It was a girl's voice, accented. American? She changed the subject. "Tell me, I heard a sheep got killed on the weekend, and no one knows by what. Is that true?"

Clutching a stack of horror books tightly to his chest, Ethan peeked around the bookcase. His boss stood facing a small, attractive woman, just inside the door.

Mark chuckled. "Yes. It happens occasionally. All a part of the country life, I'm afraid. I wouldn't let it worry you."

"Oh, I'm not worried," said the girl. "I like mysteries."

She was dressed simply, practically nondescript. Not one of those fashion-forward types, and that pleased Ethan for some reason. It was clear she cared more for what was inside than outside, though she was hardly sloppily dressed. Barely five feet tall, with black hair swept up into a bun, which made her look a bit taller, she carried herself well. But it was her eyes that gave Ethan pause. Even from here, he could see they shone. Or did they sparkle? They were definitely distinct, even behind the thin mauve-framed glasses.

She smiled. "Mystery is part of the reason I moved to England. You're full of it."

"Are we really?" Mark purred.

If the girl was offended by the supercilious undertone in Mark's voice, she made no sign. Just like his father, Old Man Glover, Mark was a bigoted idiot who felt he was above most people. But this girl, this American, there was something about her that outshone Ethan's boss. She wasn't the usual type of village airhead that got hypnotised by his money and sense of self-importance.

No, not that at all.

"Well, you'll be hearing plenty of stories from the old folk around here," Mark continued. "Especially while you're working in my shop."

Working here?

Ethan frowned. Even on a good day, there was barely enough work to keep just him busy. Most tourists came to Glastonbury for the music festival, or to see the Tor, not for books from Glover's. He knew that Mark had given this girl a job because he fancied his chances with her. He thought, arrogantly, she wouldn't be able to resist him. But, still, there was something about the American that said it would take more than money and boasts to impress her.

"Okay," she said. "Where do I begin?"

Motioning with his arm, Mark led her over to the computer on the pay desk. As she followed him, the girl smirked and looked directly into Ethan's clandestine gaze. With a start, Ethan ducked back behind the tall bookcase. He tripped, spilling his armful of books to the floor, and crashed down after them. Cursing silently, he rubbed his knee, and heard Mark say: "Ah, and that'll be the shop chimp."

"Who?"

"Ethan," Mark explained. "He helps me around here, but he's something of a village idiot, I'm afraid."

Still on the floor, Ethan stopped rubbing his knee and froze as he heard the swish of someone walking towards him. The girl's face appeared from around the bookcase.

"Hi," she said, brightly. "I'm Claire." Her smile was dazzling.

Ethan felt his face blush, and began collecting books without saying a word.

"What?" said Claire, "You're not going to say hello?"

With the books clutched to his chest, Ethan struggled to

his feet, but kept his eyes on the floor.

Mark appeared, shaking his head. "Don't mind him," he said to Claire. "He doesn't communicate well with other humans. Off you go, Ethan."

For a moment, Ethan didn't know which way to turn, and Mark laughed at him. Claire, however, did not. Finally, Ethan turned his back on the pair, and scurried from the end of the aisle.

-II-
Territory

That night, Ethan ran through Old Man Glover's wood that bordered the farmlands on the outskirts of Glastonbury. His passing barely made a sound over dead leaves and pine needles. The night was warm, the sky clear and full of sterile light. A madness, subtle and feral, blanketed Ethan, heightening his senses, his awareness, his strength. His silver pelt glowed eerily as he weaved between sturdy trees and bounded over thick, twisting roots. From somewhere, an owl hooted, lowly as if troubled. A distant bleating followed the sound.

Soon, Ethan would be amidst the docility of soft, white sheep. Fear would grip them, panicking these creatures as they smelt his presence and fled. Then, with tooth and claw, Ethan would feel the thrill of the hunt, and for the first time for at least several months, the salty taste of blood would fill his mouth. But as he ran down a decline and leapt across a narrow stream, he was suddenly aware that something was out of the ordinary. From the near distance, the sound of the sheep's agitation was already disturbing the stillness of the wood. They screamed, almost like people, and another, sharper scent filled Ethan's nostrils.

Blood had been spilt.

Coming to the edge of the wood, Ethan stopped, remaining in shadow, and surveyed the scene. Ahead, the field stretched into the gloom, and there, at the far end, the sheep had already clustered, milling and bleating, caring nothing for the barbed fence that tore at their wool. Several paces from Ethan's position was the cause of the disturbance.

A wolf sat in the field, watching Ethan with bright

yellow eyes. It was smaller than him, but with a pelt glowing no less majestically than his: a female by the scent. At her feet lay the carcass of a sheep, freshly killed. Although its whiteness was smattered with dark blood, it had not been mauled, and the wolf guarded the remains with an aura of strength and patience.

Ethan recognised her - but what was this? A challenge?

With a deep, throaty growl he padded from the tree line, and approached the intruder. She didn't move or make a sound as he neared. Ethan stopped on the opposite side of the sheep's carcass. Standing defiant, he bared his teeth and growled again.

The wolf gave a soft whine, and with slow, deliberately passive movements, manoeuvred around the carcass and approached Ethan, keeping her head lower than his at all times. He kept his pose, tense and threatening, but allowed her to smell him. She allowed herself to be smelt, inspected by Ethan, and her scent was unlike anything he had ever experienced.

Ethan barked, once, sharply, a sound half rage, half lust. The wolf backed away instantly, leaving the sheep as an offering.

Obeisance?

The aroma of sheep's blood was intoxicating, and it urged Ethan's impulses. The promise of the hunt, the kill, had vanished for the night, replaced by something new, different, by something powerful.

The intruder kept her distance as he moved to the carcass and sank long teeth through thick wool and skin, tearing free a chuck of wet meat. And in doing this, the she-wolf was pleased, accepted and accepting. Ethan growled once more, and she bounded off into the wood, leaving him to feed in peace.

-III-
A Day Off

It was Tuesday afternoon, and considering that Claire had only started working at Glover's Bookshop yesterday, she was somewhat surprised to be given the day off by her new boss. Though, in truth, Mark's interpretation of a day off was to insist Claire spend it with him so he could show her around the town she now called home. She didn't mind so much; he was still paying her, and there were worse ways to earn your money than taking a lazy stroll under the summer sun.

In truth, there wasn't much to see in Glastonbury. It was a small place, and walking from one side of the town centre to the other would take less time than it took to drink a cup of coffee. There were some quaint shops, pubs and tearooms to visit along the way - Claire was particularly taken with one shop that sold nothing but merchandise made entirely from hemp; everything, from clothes to tea – and the locals were polite and welcoming. But as small and quaint as Glastonbury was, she could understand why it was such a big tourist attraction. There was a personality about this town, a mystical quality that rose from the ground and permeated the air – something old and secret. It was the perfect place for a searching soul to discover. Claire just wished she was in better company.

As they strolled down the busy high street, Mark said, "So, you just decided to up sticks and move to England?" His voice held a tone that suggested a woman doing this all on her little lonesome was stranger than Martians invading Earth.

"It was not quite that easy," Claire replied, keeping her

voice neutral. "I moved around the States for a while, but in the end it kind of felt like I wasn't really moving at all unless I crossed an ocean."

"Yes, quite. Well, I for one am glad your itchy feet brought you to merry ol' England." This time he said it like just being in his company was reward enough for Claire's decision to leave her native country; and when he added, "There's no firmer ground than Blighty, am I right?" it suddenly dawned on her that Mark had never left England in his entire life.

In fact, the furthest he had probably ever travelled from Glastonbury was to Oxford, where he assured Claire he received the best education that money could buy. If he was supposed to be living proof of that, then Claire had her doubts. What kind of intelligent person insisted on wearing a three-piece-suit in this weather?

They came upon a line of market stalls selling various wares and foods, and Claire stopped to browse the items on a jewellery stand, where a tattooed woman with dreadlocks and dressed in purple velvet informed her that every piece on display was made from stones found in the local area.

Mark waited with obviously feigned patience, and he showed no interest in the vendor and her stall, or any other merchant in the market. Claire couldn't help but notice that they paid just as little attention to him.

What Claire had really hoped would happen today was that Mark would leave her and Ethan alone in the bookshop. She longed to speak to him about last night in the wood. Was he pleased she had left him the sheep as an offering? Or was he angry that she had so brazenly encroached onto his territory? Ethan had seemed to accept her presence, but she needed to hear him say it, to confirm it to her face. Trouble was she had yet to hear him say a single word in human form. But not to worry, Claire supposed. A face-to-face chat could wait; there were other ways to confirm his pleasure or displeasure. She'd just have to wait until after the sun went down.

"Your family must be terribly worried for you," Mark said.

"Hmm?" Claire replied absently as she studied a necklace with an amethyst pendant.

"Your family," Mark repeated. "Someone back home must be missing you right now?"

Now Claire paid attention to what he was saying, sudden ice froze in her gut, and she pretended to study the pendant more closely. "No."

Her tone was hard, but Mark seemed not to notice.

"Really? There's no one you left behind."

Shaking her head, Claire set down the necklace and picked up a black onyx ring. When she answered, she tried to keep her voice as natural as possible. "My family's gone. I'm the only one left."

"Oh, my poor dear. I'm so sorry to hear that."

It was the first time Claire had heard anything like sincerity in Mark's voice, and it sounded uncomfortable on his tongue.

"It's all right," Claire said. "I've had a long time to deal with it."

A brief moment of silence passed, during which Claire could almost hear the cogs turning in Mark's head.

"Choose something," he said, motioning to the wares of the jewellery stall. "Whatever you like. I'll pay. It'll be my gift to you."

Claire sighed inwardly. If Mark wasn't such an obvious idiot she might've been offended that he thought a simple gift of home-made jewellery could in anyway ease the pain of her life. As it was, she set the onyx ring down and gave him her sweetest smile.

"It's a generous offer, but no thank you. I prefer to pay my own way."

"Ah, a woman of independence, I see."

"You could say that."

With a nod of gratitude to the vendor, Claire stepped away from the stall, and she and Mark continued on along the high street. They strolled in silence for a while, and Claire could almost feel Mark's curiosity building up inside him.

Eventually, he said, "Claire, if it's not too rude to ask, what happened to your family?"

Claire shrugged. "There's really not much to tell," she lied. "My family had a run of . . . bad luck, I guess. Some might even say we were cursed."

"Cursed? That sounds like something the locals around here would say."

"Everywhere has locals, Mark." She snorted a small laugh, and then her expression became serious. "For a while, it was just me and my sister - Sara. But she left me alone when she died in a fire a couple of years back, and I've been looking for a home ever since."

"And now you've found one," Mark said in his best attempt at a sympathetic and comforting tone. "What happened to your parents?"

"My mom died young. So did her mom. As for my dad-" she shrugged again "-I never knew him."

"Well now . . ." It was Mark's turn to give a small laugh. "I'm afraid that gives you something in common with our Ethan."

"Really?"

"Oh yes – his family has its own tragedies. His father was just some traveller passing through Glastonbury. His mother died in childbirth, and he was raised by his grandmother - a nice old woman. Mabel was her name. But she died . . . Oh, must be ten or more years ago now."

"That's really sad," Claire said.

"Yes, I suppose it is. But Ethan didn't do so bad out of his grandmother's death. He inherited her cottage – a little rundown thing out near Father's cornfields – and rumour has it Mabel had a little money tucked away, which must be true because Ethan certainly couldn't survive on the money I pay him alone."

Mark chuckled, and his distinct lack of compassion made Claire bristle.

"I'm sure he'd give it all up to have his family back," she said.

"I wouldn't know," Mark replied offhandedly. "I can't even remember the last time I heard Ethan speak."

"Have you tried asking him?"

"Why?"

Claire bit her tongue, and Mark said nothing further, as they headed out of the high street and turned right into a narrow country lane. Here, there were a few gruff-looking farmhands sitting outside a pub called the Jack and Jenny, enjoying pints of bitter in the sunshine. A couple of them nodded to Mark, though their expressions remained noncommittal. Mark nodded back at them, and gave a smile to a wiry and hard-looking old woman collecting empty pint glasses from the tables.

"Good afternoon, Doris," Mark said. "Business booming as usual, I see."

With a stack of glasses held in her hands, a dishrag slung over her shoulder, Doris looked at Mark with the kind of glare that might've set fire to something marginally drier.

"Haven't seen your dad for a couple of days now, Mr. Glover," she said, sternly.

"Excuse me?" Mark replied, more than a little perplexed.

"Your father. He hasn't been in for a drink in awhile."

"Well . . ." Mark gave Claire an apologetic look, and then frowned at Doris. "He's been very busy, I suppose."

Doris's expression didn't alter. "Give him a message

from me, will you?"

"Yes, of course."

"Tell him a few of us would like a word with him."

"I'll pass it on, Doris."

"See that you do, Mr. Glover."

Doris turned her fiery glare onto Claire for a brief moment, and then, without so much as a goodbye or thank you, she turned and carried the stack of glasses back into the pub. The farmhands sitting at the tables looked anywhere but at Mark.

"Mad as a hatter," Mark said, mostly to himself. "Sorry about that," he said to Claire. "Shall we continue?"

But Claire wasn't listening. Something had caught her eye. In the near distance, a monument sat upon a large hill. It was a tower of some kind that pointed to the sky like a dark needle.

"What's that?" she said.

Mark followed her line of sight. "Oh, that's just Glastonbury Tor," he said.

"And that tower thing?"

"What's left of St. Michael's church."

The image of it, shimmering in the summer air, mesmerised Claire. "Can we go and see it?"

Mark pulled a face. "Not today, my dear. Not in this heat – it's a steep climb up that hill. Maybe another time."

"Okay." Claire couldn't hide the disappointment in her voice.

"I could show you the abbey instead?" Mark said quickly and brightly. "We could have a spot of lunch, and head there after."

"Actually," Claire said, still staring at the tower on the hill, "I'm pretty bushed." She looked at Mark. "I still have a touch of jetlag. I hope you don't mind."

"Oh, I see," Mark said, a little stiffly.

"I'd better head back to the hotel. But thank you for a lovely day."

"Where are you staying?"

"At the Travel Lodge – you know, just until I get my feet on the ground."

"Then let me walk you back," Mark said, hoping, no doubt, that he might get an invite into her hotel room for a lazy afternoon in her bed.

She smirked. "No, that's Okay."

"You're sure?"

"What can I tell you," she said as she began walking away. "I'm an independent woman."

-IV-
Acceptance

That night, Claire stalked the darkness, running though Old Man Glover's wood, heading towards the field of succulent sheep. Sleek and fast, she sped through the bracken like a streak as her pelt glowed as though reflecting the light of the moon. As she neared the tree line at the edge of the field, she picked up a warning scent and halted her progress. There was something alien among the sheep, a presence that filled her nostrils with the smell of cheap soap, and deodorant that did little to mask the stench of stale sweat.

If Claire so chose, she could move with the grace and silence of a summer breeze, but even she was not quick enough to dodge bullets.

In the field with the sheep, two men sat at a rickety looking camping table, playing cards in the light of a battery lamp. The older of the two was a portly, balding man; the younger was lanky with pointed features and thick glasses. They both had shotguns, resting against the backs of their camping chairs.

Sticking to the shadows of trees, Claire listened as their voices drifted to her.

"Don't see why we have to do it," complained the younger man. "I got work tomorrow."

"*Work*!" the older man scoffed. "Alls you do is sit on your bony arse in the Bobby Shop all day answering phones."

"It's an important job, I'll have you know. That's police work, that is."

"You're a receptionist, so pipe down and give me another card." The older man chuckled.

Upon the table were two opened bottles of ale, and

Claire could smell the beverage, warm and hoppy. There was also a plastic tub containing food – cheese and onion sandwiches by the scent. The flock of sheep kept their distance from the two men, huddling together with the occasional troubled bleat. Claire's gaze moved to the shotguns: one stiff breeze, one sudden change in the wind's direction, the sheep would detect her, and then she would be staring down the barrels of those weapons.

But she couldn't leave: what if Ethan came?

"All right," said the older man. "Let's see what you've got."

The younger man spread his cards on the table. "Two pair," he said, grinning broadly. "Sevens over threes."

"That's a tough one to beat," the old man said. "I've only got four jacks."

The grin fell from the younger man's face and he groaned. The older man laughed brightly.

"That's two more squids you owe me," he said, happily, and he scooped up the cards. "My deal."

As the cards were shuffled, the younger man started complaining again.

"I still don't see what's got the old man's knickers in a twist. I mean, he don't bother spending nights out here like us, do he?"

The older man stopped mid-shuffle. "Watch that gip, boy," he warned. "Glover's been good to this town over the years. If he says something needs doing, it gets done. No questions."

"But sheep being eaten by *monsters*?"

Claire's ears pricked up.

The older man made an angry noise and resumed shuffling. "Your trouble is you're too young and stupid to see past the crumpet that walks around town with all their bits hanging out of their short skirts. But I'm old, boy, and I remember the last time a monster roamed these fields."

The younger man scoffed. "You don't believe that old werewolf bollocks, do you? Even Glover's son laughs at the idea."

"Glover's son ain't much different from you."

"Then he's got his head screwed on right, ain't he? Left up to me, I'd take a trip to the pig farm and have a word with Parcy. His dogs escape all the time, and vicious buggers they are, too. I bets it's them what's bothering the sheep."

"I wish you were right, boy," the older man said. "But Old Man Glover's rarely wrong, and I reckon there's a hunt coming soon."

He began dealing the cards, and the younger man shook his head at his friend, and helped himself to a sandwich from the tub.

Claire felt a thrill as her taste buds plucked a new scent from the air as easily as she might catch a butterfly in a net: blood and fear. She backed away into the wood, realising that she needn't have worried about Ethan; this was his territory, and of course he would know there men with guns guarding the sheep.

She crept deeper into the trees, picking up speed as she dodged between shafts of moonlight and shadows. The salty tang of blood grew stronger and stronger, and the pull of a fresh kill led Claire to a clearing. Her heart hammered. There, powerful and confident, sat Ethan, his pelt radiating sliver, glowing just like hers. His muzzle was matted with blood, and at his feet was a deer – dead with its throat ripped clean away.

Ethan was waiting, offering her the chance to feed with him, but respect for his territory still had to be shown. Head low, Claire loped into the clearing and laid down several feet from the wolf and the deer.

Ethan snorted: satisfaction. He sank his teeth into the deer's flank, ripped free a chunk of flesh, and ate it with noisy smacks. The smell of fresh blood was heady, and

Claire whined her eagerness. Ethan finished his mouthful, and then gave a short, low bark: permission.

With her head still bowed, Claire moved forward, careful not to go too fast. Ethan sat still and proud as she licked the blood from his muzzle. With a gentle nudge, he urged Claire to eat, and she gratefully sank her teeth into the soft, warm meat of the deer. Together they fed.

-V-
Promise of the Hunt

Wednesday afternoon arrived, and Mark decided that it was the perfect time for him and Claire to have a long lunch as the Jack and Jenny pub. The bar was quiet: a few local farmers, in for a lunchtime pint or two, stood at the bar chatting with Doris, the elderly and severe-looking landlady. Claire and Mark sat away from the group, at a small table by a window, waiting for their food order. Outside, summer bathed the streets in sunlight, the gardens of houses bloomed with bright colours, but Claire felt as though it was cold, cloudy and damp.

Listening to Mark had become like listening to a doll with a drawstring voice box. It wasn't so much *what* he said, but the *way* he said it. The volume of his voice was always set slightly too loud, remaining at the same whining pitch, and his smug expression suggested he thought he knew something no else did, whatever the topic. On and on he droned, and Claire wondered how he would react if she were to suddenly jab a fork into his forehead.

". . . But when all's said and done," Mark blustered, "Father's a shrewd businessman, even if he is a superstitious old fart – excuse my French."

He chuckled. Claire smiled and sipped her wine. Her gaze travelled to the fork lying beside the placemat on the table. She refrained from temptation and nodded interestedly as Mark continued.

"Of course, with me as his son he can't stand to fail. Father has all the experience, but I have all the brains, and . . ."

Blah, blah, blah was all Claire heard.

Still nodding, still smiling, she sipped her wine some

more, forced her mind to drown out Mark's voice, and let her thoughts wander.

As a human being, Ethan had no social skills. That much was becoming obvious. Claire had really hoped that today would be the day she finally got to talk with him. But, of course, Mark hadn't left her side all morning, and Ethan had remained hidden in the bookracks. She had hardly caught a glimpse of him. It was as if he was deliberately avoiding her, and not just because of his taciturn nature. She couldn't understand why. Not after what they had shared.

But what truly bemused Claire was the way Ethan let Mark push him about. Mark was a bully, pure and simple, and he enjoyed ridiculing his employee to the point where Claire wondered if the only reason he kept him around was to sate his own spiteful amusement. Ethan never stuck up for himself, never stood his ground or answered back. At best he would mumble some weak and unintelligible noise of submission before shuffling off to disappear among the racks of books once again. It infuriated Claire. Why couldn't he show his boss just a little of the strength that she had witnessed under the moonlight, where the scrawny introvert became a true master of his domain?

Perhaps he would with Claire's help, for it was under the cover of darkness where the two of them really communicated, where a relationship was blossoming perfectly. On the first night, Claire had hunted food for Ethan, and shown respect for his territory; last night, he had hunted food for Claire, and given her permission to stay; and tonight . . . tonight they would-

"Any chance of some food, Doris?" Mark called out way too loudly, disturbing the landlady's conversation with the farmers, along with Claire's thoughts. "We've been waiting over half-an-hour now!"

Doris scowled over at the table, and Claire hid behind her wineglass.

"Shouldn't be long now, Mr. Glover," she said, flatly.

"I should hope not," Mark replied. "Not exactly busy, are you?" Shaking his head, he faced Claire again.

Over at the bar, Doris rolled her eyes and pursed her lips. The farmers pulled faces at each other and sniggered. Claire was heartened to realise that she was not the only one who thought Mark was a total asshole. This revelation was worth the downside of these people thinking that she was nothing but Mark's latest score.

"Now, where the bloody hell was I?" Mark said.

Claire shrugged. "Your father?"

"Ah, yes," he said, brightly, and took a sip of his wine. "There are a lot of stories about him, you know. When I was just a boy, they say he hunted down some kind of animal that was terrorising Glastonbury, killing livestock and whatnot."

Claire's interest picked up. "The mysterious monster," she said.

"Ah, I see you've been infected by the parochial mindset." Mark chuckled. "Understand, my dear, Glastonbury is steeped in old stories and legends, superstitions that are used to encourage the tourist trade. That, and the music festival is all that puts us on the map.

"As for monsters roaming our lands – utter bunkum, I'm afraid, just like the myths of King Arthur."

"I believe in King Arthur," Claire said with her sweetest smile. "And I believe in monsters. What makes you so sure your father didn't catch one?"

Mark pulled a dubious face. "You're honestly trying to defend some over-inflated story concerning a *werewolf*?"

"Sure. Why not?"

"Well, really!" Mark chuckled some more. "This is real life, Claire, not some *American* movie."

Claire shrugged. "All myths and stories have some

truth behind them."

"True, I suppose," Mark conceded. "Oh, I'm certain that the villagers once took the law into their own hands, led by Father, of course. And I've no doubt they did hunt a *type* of monster, and used the werewolf myth as an excuse." He sighed. "But it was probably some criminal or pervert from out of town, and even the police turned a blind eye when he disappeared. Good for them, if you ask me. Sometimes the law is found wanting, and matters need to be dealt with in a more . . . *local* fashion. Am I right?"

"Oh, absolutely," Claire said, thoughtfully. "But you never asked your father about it? I mean, about the werewolf?"

"Good lord no," Mark scoffed. "A conversation with Father is tedious enough at the best of times. But to give him the opportunity to prattle on with old stories – no, no, no – he'd never shut up!"

Claire gave her best, politest smile. "Then tell me something else: who's Parcy?"

Mark eyed her for a short moment. "Have you been listening to the gossips, my dear?"

"I overheard someone mention his name, if that's what you mean. Something about dogs?"

Mark sat back in his chair, and sucked air over his teeth. "Bill Parcy. He runs Father's pig farm. He owns three big Rottweilers, and they truly are the Hounds of Hell. The only person who can control them is Parcy himself. He makes sure they cause no harm . . . for the most part."

"So you think dogs are killing the sheep?" Claire said.

"Seems likely, and it wouldn't be the first time." There was a small degree of genuine remorse in Mark's voice. "The trouble is, Bill Parcy has no relatives, no wife or children. His dogs are his world. If they were taken away from him, he'd have nothing left. Even Father is reluctant to do that to him."

At that moment, Doris appeared carrying two plates of food. She thumped the plates down onto the table, and Claire looked at her roast beef sandwich, and the pile of greasy, finger-fat chips that seemed to accompany every meal in England. Claire smiled at Doris and thanked her. Mark mumbled something about it being about time, and scrapped the onions from his sausage baguette. He paused and looked at Doris, who seemed to be making a point of not leaving him alone.

"Something you want, Doris?" Mark said, as if there was nothing on Earth he and this old landlady could have in common.

"Another one last night, Mr. Glover," Doris said. "That's three in three nights now."

Mark looked at Claire with a confused expression, and then back at Doris. "What on Earth are you talking about, woman?"

Doris glared. "The groundsmen found a deer this morning, out in your dad's wood. Ripped to pieces it was."

Claire froze, and Mark's face darkened.

"Not an entirely appropriate lunchtime conversation, is it, Doris?" he said.

The landlady shifted her gaze to Claire, and narrowed her eyes. Although Claire liked the fact that Doris was imperially unimpressed by Mark's manner, her stare was fierce, like her stony eyes could cut through any bullshit and façade to see the truth, and Claire had to look away lest Doris saw what lurked behind her mauve glasses.

She picked up her beef sandwich like it was a shield.

"What's your father going to do about it?" Doris said to Mark.

"I don't know," Mark replied. "Why don't you ask *him*?"

"Maybe I will." Doris snorted. "You were just a lad the last time it happened, Mr. Glover." She cut Claire with her sharp eyes once more. "But I remember all too well."

With that, she strode away, and slipped back behind the bar, where she began cleaning glasses and muttering under her breath with a face like thunder.

"Brilliant!" Mark snapped, and he threw a paper napkin onto his untouched food. "People have been living in this area for more than ten-thousand years, and you'd think they would have learned to curb their hysteria by now." He rose from his chair. "This situation needs bringing to an end before Father has the whole village crying 'werewolf'." He took his wallet from his pocket, and laid a twenty-pound note on the table. "Forgive me, my dear, but I have to cut lunch short and pay Bill Parcy a visit."

"No problem," Claire said through a mouthful of sandwich. "I'll meet you back at the shop?"

"No, no – you might as well take the rest of the day off. I'll see you tomorrow."

And with that, Mark left the Jack & Jenny in a grim mood.

Immediately finding herself in better company, Claire's mood brightened. Twenty pounds was far more than enough to pay for lunch, but then Doris deserved a big tip for her services. Claire finished her sandwich with relish; she needed to keep up her strength for the hunt tonight.

-VI-
Abstinence

St. Michael's church stood as a sentinel atop Glastonbury Tor, like the sole remaining tower of a castle that had long ceased to exist. It was hollow inside, and Ethan looked up the length of its interior, and out through the open roof, to gaze upon the moon, a blurred patch of silver in the cloudy night sky.

Some said that the Tor and the tower marked the location of the entrance to the underworld; others believed it was the doorway to mythical Avalon. If either were true, if such a doorway presented itself at that moment, Ethan would have gladly stepped through and left this world forever.

He walked out of the tower, onto the hillside, and looked down at the lights of Glastonbury far below. The town seemed so small from this height, hemmed in by Old Man Glover's expansive lands. The fresh wind whipped Ethan's thin T-shirt, and brought a bitterness that bit deep despite the night's humidity.

Instinctively, Ethan knew what was expected of him next. On this third night, he and Claire were supposed to join and experience the ecstasy of the hunt together. No doubt she was already out there, in Old Man Glover's wood, waiting for him, prepared and eager. But Ethan wouldn't incite the metamorphosis, wouldn't run with Claire. Not tonight; it was too dangerous.

Ethan's grandmother had always taught him to be sensible, careful to control his urges, to steer clear of villagers as he ran free at night. It was all right, she would say, once in a very rare while to hunt and kill a deer or sheep; but only enough to sate his urges, to give the townsfolk a little mystery, never so much as to induce panic. After she died, leaving her grandson alone in the little cottage, Ethan never forgot her lessons, and lived by them each day.

As a wolf, he had always felt so strong and confident. Never once had the weakling he was by day invaded his nights. Until Claire came. She made Ethan question everything. She had come to him as a kindred spirit, paid respect, asked to be let in . . . and now Ethan had to slam the door in her face. It was safer that way.

Only Old Man Glover and his generation aired their superstitions, and they were a dwindling bunch. But now Claire had given him good reason to inflame the locals. Ethan had allowed her to draw too much attention to their hunts; they had killed too many nights in a row now.

It was courage he lacked, courage to speak with Claire during the day. England wasn't big like America; people noticed everything, especially here in a small town like Glastonbury. If only he was strong enough to explain that to her, to make her see. But Claire both frightened and exited him in more ways than he could understand.

Ethan froze as a howl echoed across Glastonbury from somewhere distant. It was a sound full of frustration, of anger, and it seemed to encourage the wind's fierceness around the Tor. He closed his eyes and a single tear leaked onto his cheek. If he and Claire were to be together, then she would have to learn patience.

-VII-
Last Chance

The next morning in Glover's Bookshop, Claire struggled to maintain a calm façade. Ethan was hiding out among the bookcases as usual, and she wanted nothing more than to confront him, shout at him, strangle him as she demanded some explanations of why he abandoned her last night; but once again, Mark would not leave her side, and the monotony of his voice was like the turning of a slow drill in her temple.

"I've an idea," Mark said. "Why don't we take the day off tomorrow? I could take you to Cheddar Gorge. It's a beautiful place. We could spend the day looking around the gift shops and exploring the caves. What do you say?"

"Sounds great," Claire replied, and smiled as Mark droned on about a cheese factory, quaint pubs and tea rooms, and an apparently charming fish and chips restaurant.

No doubt Mark thought he could impress Claire enough to get into her underwear, but in reality that was as likely to happen as a sheep learning to bleat 'The Star Spangled Banner'. She hadn't come to Glastonbury looking for romance with a spoilt and arrogant farmer's son; but the person Claire did came here to see had now turned out to be a disloyal idiot. It was as if Ethan wasn't even in the shop . . . but he was there, somewhere, lurking among the bookracks, not making a sound. Claire could smell him.

"Or maybe you'd prefer a trip to Bath to see the Roman ruins?" Mark said, but before Claire could answer, the phone rang. Disgruntled, he snatched it up. "Hello . . .?" His face fell, and he placed a hand over the receiver. "Sorry, my dear," he whispered. "I really have to take this."

Claire nodded understandingly.

"What can I do for you, Father?" Mark said into the phone. "Excuse me . . .? Another one? *Three!* You're not serious?"

Claire averted her eyes. It was obvious they were talking about the unguarded sheep she had killed last night. It was a senseless slaughter, an angry reaction to Ethan's rejection.

"What . . .?" said Mark. "Yes, yes I went to see Bill Parcy yesterday . . . I don't care if I upset him. If he can't keep those damned dogs under control – what . . .? Yes, I know he says they haven't been out, but he'd say anything to protect those bloody things. One of them almost bit me while I was there." He rolled his eyes at Claire.

In return, Claire gave a tight smile, mouthed the words, "I'll leave you to it", and took the chance to slip away, to move into the bookcases.

Ethan was hiding in the Science section. He stiffened visibly when he noticed Claire approaching him. He didn't turn to face her, and she moved in front of him with a defiant glare. He wouldn't meet her eyes, and tried to shuffle off, clutching a huge *Book of the Universe* to his chest as though it was the only thing protecting him. Claire grabbed the bookcase, and used her arm to block his path.

"Look at me," she whispered hoarsely.

Ethan looked to his feet.

"Why didn't you meet me last night?"

Silence.

Claire took a calming breath. "Do you think I'm weak?" she said. "Do you think I submit to just anyone?" Still Ethan gave no response. "I came to you in good faith. I respected your territory. You accepted me. You let me share your food. We were going places. But now you can't even look at me?" She gripped his arm. "I've searched a long time for someone like you, Ethan, someone like me. But I won't be treated like this, you hear?"

Although Ethan remained silent, Claire felt his arm muscle tense. She kept her hand in place - a show of strength, a challenge.

In the background, Mark's raised voice rang out. "All right, Father! Have it your way! I'll round up the boys, if that's what you want!"

"Listen to me," Claire hissed, shaking Ethan. "We need each other. But I won't submit again, not unless you meet me halfway."

The air was filled with the harsh ringing sound of Mark slamming the phone down. "Bloody old fart!" he shouted.

"This is your last chance," Claire told Ethan. "You either talk to me or I'm gone in the morning. Got it?"

For the first time, Ethan looked up. His eyes glinted, wet and round. Was it fear Claire saw? She released his arm. Ethan's lips trembled and opened as if he was about say something, but Mark appeared and interrupted the moment.

"Ethan," he snapped. "Leave Claire alone and get on with some bloody work."

Ethan mumbled an unintelligible response, and shuffled off. As he disappeared into another aisle, his weak subservience drove a knife into Claire's gut.

Mark chuckled and shook his head. "That was almost a coherent sentence," he called after Ethan. "Very well done."

Claire did her best to smile as Mark turned to her.

"That was Father," he said, and sighed. "More sheep have been killed, and his superstitions have run a little wild, I'm afraid. He's organising a monster hunt."

"A hunt?" Claire said, blurting the words.

"Yes. He wants me to round up the farmhands and groundsmen for a meeting at the Jack & Jenny tonight."

Mark shook his head, clearly believing his father was wasting everybody's time. "You'll come, won't you? It'll be a good opportunity to soak up some of those parochial eccentricities that entertain you so much."

Claire forced her smile. "Wouldn't miss it for the world."

-VIII-
Isolation

The Jack & Jenny was a popular pub among the locals of Glastonbury, an old and smoky place where everybody knew everybody, but where tourists rarely bothered to frequent. At the weekends, it always stayed open beyond the closing time decreed by English drinking laws, but Doris, the landlady, never got into trouble for this misdemeanour, as some of her best customers were members of the local police.

But here and now, Ethan couldn't remember seeing the Jack & Jenny filled with so many drinkers on a week night.

Sitting, as always, at a small corner table away from the main crowd, Ethan sipped at a pint in solitude. At the back of the bar, some of the younger patrons played pool as they laughed and drank. The boys boasted to the girls, secure in their masculinity, and for the most part, the girls pretended to be impressed. In the main bar, the older men converged with a distinct lack of wives: a consortium of townsfolk from strong farmhands to elderly groundsmen and shopkeepers.

Some looked grim, clutching pint glasses tightly, and talking in clandestine whispers. Some seemed more cheery, enjoying the expectant atmosphere. Doris served a drink to the police sergeant across a bar strewn with shotguns, cracked open and unloaded - at least for the time being - and here and there, propped up against the walls, were a few farm tools, scythes and pitchforks, like a scene from an old horror film. The chatter of voices was like a swarm of angry insects.

All these people, they were here on the orders of one man. He stood at the bar, like a king considering his subjects. Stout and ruddy-faced, he wore a tweed suit and a stern expression; his hair was grey, with huge sideburns shaped like lamb chops, and as neat and tidy as his thick moustache. A host of sycophants busied around him, listening to his blustery voice as though he spoke the words of a sage. Old Man Glover was a cornerstone of Glastonbury, and when he spoke, everybody listened.

But Ethan was not here on the command of Mark's father. His drink barely touched, he played with a beer-mat, searching inside for courage enough to do what his heart most wanted.

I'm gone in the morning, Claire had said, and those words bounced around Ethan's head.

At that moment, the pub door opened, followed by a voice as loud and boastful as its sire's. Mark Glover stepped in, still trying his best to impress a small, pretty American girl.

". . . But of course, he was no match-" Mark was interrupted by a booming voice.

"Where the bloody hell have you been?" said Old Man Glover.

Mark peered defiantly across the now silent pub, and raised an eyebrow at his father. "I was escorting Claire to the meeting, if it's all the same to you."

"Damn boy!" his father rumbled. "Get over here. Now!"

Mark rolled his eyes at Claire, and then led her by the hand towards his father. As she moved past him, Claire spared Ethan a cursory glance, and then looked away.

Ethan looked down into his beer, and dug deep, praying that he could find the strength to beg Claire not to leave.

-IX-
In the Court of the Old Man

Claire felt somewhat intimidated to be under the scrutiny of so many people she didn't know, and every set of eyes seemed to follow her as Mark led her across the bar floor. She did her best to ignore the stares, but found it much easier to ignore Ethan. The truth was she had all but given up on him. This was his last chance to talk to her; there was no other reason why she would come here to listen to these old farts prattle on about monsters and hunts. But her heart was sinking fast. Deep down, she knew if Ethan wanted her around, he would have talked to her by now, no matter how shy and inept he was. He wouldn't have left her stranded in the wood.

Tomorrow, she would have to leave Glastonbury and continue her search. She was beginning to wonder why she had bothered to come to this meeting at all.

"Father, this is Claire," Mark said as they came to stand before the fabled Old Man Glover.

He regarded her with unashamed suspicion and irritation in his bloodshot eyes. His grizzled face was stony, hardened by years of intolerance.

"She's from America," Mark continued. "I've given her a job at the bookshop."

"So I've been told," Glover said with a broad local accent. With no further acknowledgement to Claire's presence, he turned his stern gaze to his son. "And you decided to bring a girl here? Tonight?"

"Obviously, Father," Mark replied, dryly. "Claire has an interest in local customs."

"And no doubt you've an interest in the colour of her knickers."

"Father, please!"

As a few of Glover's cronies chuckled at his comments and the embarrassment they caused his son, Claire decided to interject.

"If I might, sir," she said. "Mark has been nothing but a gentleman. And I'm not here to interfere with your hunt. It's no place for someone like me, right?" And mentally, she added, *you misogynistic old bastard.*

Glover looked her up and down, and said, "I'm afraid my son doesn't respect the world as I do, Miss Claire. There are certain things that he refuses to believe to his own detriment."

"Like the existence of monsters," Mark scoffed loudly, as though passing judgement on every person present.

But his supercilious expression was cut dead by his father's cold glare.

"You're an embarrassment to me, boy," he said, his voice full of menace and warning. "Maybe you'll learn a thing or two tonight. I only hope it's not the hard way, though God knows you deserve it sometimes."

Tight-jawed, Mark was unable to hold his father's eyes - or Claire's. "I'm here, aren't I?" he grumbled like a scolded schoolboy. "I did as you asked. Isn't that enough?"

But the old man wasn't to be placated. "I blame your mother," he said with harsh regret. "She put the soft touch in you."

Keeping his eyes low, Mark replied, "And what did *you* ever do for me, Father, apart from criticise?" and a sudden hush descended in the pub.

No one sniggered now, and all eyes looked anywhere but at the father and son as Old Man Glover's already ruddy face turned an angrier shade of red. Every person who had been enjoying Mark's public dressing-down knew as a collective that he had stepped over a line. Claire resisted the urge to back away from the situation, and almost felt sorry for Mark; he, too, knew he had gone too far, and he seemed to shrink as his father appeared to swell like a gathering storm.

Thankfully, it was a strong, no-nonsense voice from behind the bar that disturbed the menacing silence.

"Now then, Mr. Glover – you can't always blame the woman," Doris said. "A boy's got to take responsibility for himself eventually, else he don't become a man, see?"

To Claire's surprise, the old man gave the landlady an approving nod. "Wisely spoken, Doris," he said, and then poked his son in the chest. "What do you say, *boy*? Think you can act like a man for the night?"

Claire could sense the anger growing in Mark, and despite his obvious fear of his father, he looked as though he might reach out and snap the finger that just poked him. Instead, he turned an accusing glare to Doris.

"Don't look at me like that," the landlady said with a roll of her eyes and a shake of her head. "If you were mine, I'd have orphaned you off a long time ago."

This comment broke the tension, and chuckles filled the pub again, though more from relief than genuine amusement.

Mark's shoulders sagged with resignation, and he looked pathetic.

"Why don't you tell your son's American friend why we're here, Mr. Glover," Doris added, as the general drone and hum of voices began to arise again. She fixed her sharp eyes onto Claire. "She might not truly realise what she's got herself involved in."

"Excellent idea, Doris," Glover said. With his eyes on Claire, he called out to a policeman standing at the bar wearing a sergeant's uniform. "How long since the last time, Reg?"

"Thirty years, give or take," the policeman answered, staring down into his pint of dark beer.

"And that wasn't the first time, was it?"

"No, Mr. Glover, not by any means."

The old man gave Claire a crooked, humourless smile. "You see, Miss Claire, most of us here have lived in this town all our lives, and despite what my son might say, we know monsters are real. I remember them from my youth. So did my father, and his father . . ."

Claire listened with polite interest as she was regaled with tales of Glastonbury's grisly past. She was told in no uncertain terms that a monster, half-wolf, half-human, returned to Glastonbury every generation or so. All though no one said as much, it was obvious to Claire that many of the men present had hunted the beast the last time it was around, and a few of them were quick to add their own tales and theories to the conversation.

Some said it was the magic in the ground that drew the wolves to Glastonbury; others believed it was the same monster, reincarnated into every generation, which caused Claire to wonder if the wolf had always been in Ethan's family line. She glanced over at him and sighed inwardly as she saw he was still sitting at the corner table, but had now turned his back on the rest of the pub.

The evening wore on, and Mark managed to shrug off his earlier embarrassment and return to his normal blustery and over-opinionated self. A few of the younger drinkers left the pub, and a few late stragglers arrived, who seemed even more eager than those already in attendance to join the hunt. Claire struggled to quell her rising anxiety. A frenzy was slowly building here, and she realised how dangerous it was to remain in Glastonbury, especially with Old Man Glover stoking the local fire. Did Ethan realise that too?

". . . And I'm telling you, boy," the old man was saying pointedly to his son, "if this was a wild dog, we'd have caught it by now." He looked at Claire. "The shame of it is - I've no desire to lead a hunt. If the monster left

Glastonbury by itself, I'd let it go, and good riddance to it. Let someone else deal with the problem. But it won't move on. No. It's got a taste for blood now, and it's only a matter of time before it comes for one of us, see?"

Mark, utterly perplexed by these words, looked about to give a retort when his attention was captured by someone brushing past him and Claire to place an empty pint glass on the bar top.

"Ethan!" Mark called, glibly. "I didn't know you were here. You're not joining the hunt, are you?" Judging by his expression, the very idea of this amused Mark deeply.

Ethan looked at his feet and shook his head.

"I thought as much," Mark said. "Courage really isn't your strong point, is it?"

Claire could have wept as Ethan just stood there and took these comments, along with the chuckles they induced from those around him. Even Old Man Glover seemed amused by Ethan's presence, shaking his head as he turned and ordered another whiskey from Doris.

But then, to Claire's surprise, Ethan looked up at Mark, and said, "I'm meeting a friend."

"A friend?" Mark said, doing nothing to hide his astonishment at hearing Ethan speak so coherently. He snorted a laugh. "That's doubtful, but I don't really care. Off you go, Ethan."

As Mark turned his back, Ethan looked directly into Claire's eyes. "Hi," he said, and walked away.

Her heart beating hard, Claire watched him leave the Jack and Jenny without a backward glance. She then flinched as Old Man Glover's voice boomed out, addressing the whole pub.

"A toast to you all," he said, holding his whiskey high. "You know why we're here. Let's make no bones about it . . ."

Claire didn't listen to the rest. She turned to Mark and smiled. "Your father's right," she said. "This is no place for a girl. I'll leave you boys to it."

Mark nodded and frowned. "I'll walk you home."

"No, no," Claire said. "I'm fine. I'll see you at work."

And before he could object, she headed off, weaving between the clustered drinkers, towards the door. She looked back from the threshold to see Mark frowning after her. She gave him a quick smile, and then realised that he wasn't the only one watching her. From behind the bar, Doris was glowering. Claire turned from the landlady's fierce eyes, and stepped out into the hot night.

At first, there was no sign of Ethan. She sniffed at the air, her superior senses piercing through the scent of burnt sausage and rancid ale, the scent of dry wood and earth, and she found his smell. There he was! Just up ahead, Ethan was waiting in the shadows wrought by moonlight and a broken street lamp.

Claire headed straight for him. As she approached, he began fidgeting, stepping from foot-to-foot, as though struggling to find the words he so desperately wanted to say to her. Claire didn't break her gait. She grabbed his shoulders and pulled him into a kiss. A long, sensuous kiss.

-X-
Contact

The sight of her face so close to his, the smell of her skin, the taste of her tongue in his mouth, the sound of her groan, and the feel of her body against his . . .

Ethan almost howled his lust.

The kiss was disturbed by the sound of raised voices, angry and eager. Reluctantly, Ethan pulled away from Claire and looked back down the road to the Jack and Jenny. No one exited the pub, but obviously Old Man Glover was fuelling the rage of his people, and the hunt would soon begin.

"Come on," Ethan whispered as he took Claire's hand. "This way-"

He led her through the back alleys and side lanes of Glastonbury. She laughed as they ran - a laugh that was full of freedom and joy. They drew strange looks from the few people they passed, and Ethan pulled Claire along harder; he found no laughter inside himself, only fear and a desperate need to be somewhere secluded where it was just the two of them.

Eventually, they reached the outskirts of town, where the expanse of Old Man Glover's cornfields stretched into the moonlit distance, full and tall and almost ready for harvest. He led Claire down a short track that cut between a grove of sycamore trees, and they came to the small cottage that Ethan called home.

He looked at Claire shyly from the corner of his eye as he slid the key into the lock and opened the front door. She was grinning as she followed him inside. With the only light source coming from the moon shining through the window, they faced each other, breathing hard from the excursion of their run. Claire's face held a sheen of sweat; Ethan's T-shirt stuck to his damp back.

"I don't want you to leave," he blurted, and willed himself to keep his eyes locked onto Claire's. They crinkled behind those mauve-framed spectacles as she smiled. "But we have to be careful," he added. "We've drawn too much attention to ourselves, and-"

"Kiss me," Claire said, hoarsely. "If you really want me to stay, kiss me now."

Ethan paused, his stomach fluttered, and then he stepped forward, cupping Claire's face and bringing their lips together. Softly at first, and then pressing harder, opening, and her tongue met his.

Claire broke the kiss, and her voice was breathy when she spoke. "I need to freshen up."

His heart thumping, his head spinning, Ethan gestured to a door on the right, halfway between the kitchen and the front door.

"The bathroom," he said, dumbly.

Claire giggled and headed towards it. "Why don't you get us some drinks."

Ethan nodded, waited until she had closed the door and locked it, and then he dashed to his bedroom.

He switched on a bedside lamp, tore the sweaty T-shirt from his body, and grabbed a fresh one. First, checking his deodorant was still working, he pulled the clean T-shirt on, and then tried to do something with his unruly hair in the mirror. He gave up, as he always did. Besides, Claire had seen him often enough; she knew what he looked like, and accepted it.

Drinks, he wondered as he entered the kitchen and switched on the light. Did she mean beer or scotch? Tea or coffee? Water or Milk? What did people drink in these situations?

In the corner of the kitchen, on the countertop beside the kettle, Ethan spied a bottle of red wine. Mark had given it to him as a staff present last Christmas. He boasted it was a good wine - a *Bordeaux*. Not that Ethan could tell the difference between a good or bad wine – they all tasted like vinegar to him. The truth was, he hadn't known what to do with Mark's gift, and it had been sitting in the kitchen, unopened and gathering dust, since the day he gave it to him. But he knew what to do with it now.

He took two wineglasses from the cupboard and washed them clean of dust before setting them down. Scrabbling around in the cutlery draw, he found a corkscrew and proceeded to screw it into the bottle's cork.

As the cork slid free with a satisfying pop, Ethan felt a sudden flush of happiness. It was an alien feeling, but one he embraced. He and Claire were safe, together, away from prying eyes and gossiping tongues, and far, far from the hunt.

-XI-
Communication

Claire had expected to be taken to some rundown shack that was a refuge for rubbish and dirt and all the other signs of a man who cared nothing for cleanliness. She most certainly didn't expect Ethan's home to smell so clean and appear so tidy. But who was he keeping it tidy for? Himself? Had he ever had a woman over before? Come to that, had Ethan even *been* with a woman before? It seemed doubtful, and Claire wondered if he learned his housekeeping skills from his grandmother, and continued them on after she died and left this homely cottage to him.

She chided herself. It was such a small matter; there were bigger things on her mind than Ethan's living habits, a thousand things that swirled and danced in her heart.

She stood in front of the bathroom mirror, staring at her reflection. She looked a mess, she realised: her clothes creased and damp with sweat; her eyes darker and more deep set than usual, and that annoying discoloration beneath her lower lids - she looked sallow and forlorn.

Her bun, a neat but hardly fashionable way to wear her hair, was now bedraggled with tendrils of dark curls sticking out and hanging loose like the springs of some broken clockwork toy. That long, black, unruly hair – wild hair, her family's hair. Her grandmother's hair. Her mother's hair. Her sister's . . .

Claire stifled a sob and closed her eyes as her head was filled with memories from a bleak past.

They never found her grandmother's body. Her mother – they said it was an accident. But her sister . . . Oh, she remembered her sister. She remembered hiding in the wood, too terrified to move as they tied Sara to the pyre, too horror-struck to run and find help as they built the wood high about her. A coward, Claire had done nothing but watch as her sister's own husband put the torch to the pyre, and the flames had reached high. The sound of the crowd's jeers and Sara's screams still haunted her sleep.

Claire opened her eyes and wiped tears from her cheeks with angry movements from her hands. Now? She had to torture herself in this way *now*? She could hear Ethan outside, clinking around, and it was the sound of the future, of something new, of hope. She could not let memories of the past ruin that.

She took off her glasses and splashed cold water on her face. It was refreshing, but did little to cool her down. She picked her glasses up, but didn't put them on again. She didn't even need to wear them. She thought they made her look intelligent or something. Or maybe they were just another layer to hide behind.

Claire glared at the bedraggled woman that stared at her from the mirror. The haunted woman. This was the look of one bearing years of grief from a centuries-old curse, a family curse that was wrought upon her face in every line, feature and detail.

How could she possibly tell Ethan why she came to England? The reason why she had been searching for someone like him for so long? He would think her a stalker - or worse, what if he really didn't want her in *that* way? Perhaps that was why Ethan hadn't beckoned to her when they were both in wolf form. He wasn't attracted to her as a woman or as a supernatural being!

No, she consoled herself. Things had already gone too far for that to be in doubt.

She had just assumed that when she met someone like Ethan he would have been searching for someone like her for just as long: someone to love and be loved by; someone to comfort and be comforted by; but most of all, someone who understood what it was to be as they were.

She hadn't expected him to be so sheltered and inexperienced – to be such a lone wolf. Claire felt certain in her heart that she was offering him everything he never realised he wanted until now.

But she had never been this stupid, this impulsive and foolish, before. Ethan was right – she had drawn too much attention to them. Where was her usual, careful practicality? The lessons learned from her mother and grandmother? Both had been pragmatic women who had carefully continued the family line while preserving its secrets of the wolf. But even they had been found out eventually, and Claire needed to take better care. She owed it to the family's bloodline.

She was ovulating now. She could feel the searing heat of it taking control of her mind and emotions, but most of all, her body, which writhed beneath the surface of her sensitive skin. But was her desire for Ethan born from lust, love or desperation?

Did it matter?

She flinched as Ethan's muffled voice came through the bathroom door.

"Are you all right in there?" he asked.

"I'm fine," Claire replied, hoping she sounded confident.

"I found some wine. It's red."

"Oh, good!" She cringed at the pseudo chirpiness in her voice. "I'll be right out."

As she listened to Ethan shuffling away from the door, she stared back at her reflection. Already the sheen of sweat had returned to her face, and her body felt hotter, stickier than ever. The summer night was so humid! How could she hope to make herself presentable in this heat?

Claire felt an angry flush. "No more layers," she whispered, and a glow began to emanate from her eyes. "No more hiding."

She dropped her glasses into the bathroom sink, and began pulling the ties and clips from her hair until the dark tendrils hung about her shoulders, as wild and natural as the scent of her skin. She cocked her head to one side and gritted her teeth as she began to unbutton her blouse.

Ethan waited for her in the kitchen, two glasses of red wine in his hands. His eyes widened and his mouth worked silently as Claire sauntered towards him wearing not one stitch of clothing. Naked, bare, she couldn't remember ever feeling this strong and confident. As she neared Ethan, she could smell his sweat. His nervousness. She sniffed again . . . Was that fear? Of her?

"You look . . . you look . . . you-" he gave up on the sentence and swallowed, hard.

"I look what, Ethan?" Claire took a wine glass from his shaking hand, and downed its contents in one go. The wine burned her tongue and throat, and she threw the empty glass over her shoulder. The sound of shattering glass brought a crooked grin to her mouth.

She stepped closer and closer to Ethan until he was backed up against the counter, and her body was pressed against his. Only the thin layer of his clothes truly separated them now.

The small but racing thumps of Ethan's heart beat upon her breast. Yes, he was fearful, she realised, but of his desire, his inexperience. He wanted Claire, and even though she had made such an obvious show of offering herself to him, he still didn't know how to take her.

A breath lodged in his throat as she licked his neck, tasting the salt in the sweat on his skin. His wine glass smashed on the kitchen floor as it slipped his grasp, and Claire's bare feet and legs were spattered with dark, blood-red wine.

She faced him again, staring into his eyes, and brought her lips within brushing distance of his.

"I want you, Ethan," she whispered. "If you'll have me..."

His eyes began to glow, and his expression changed. With one smooth motion, he lifted Claire into his arms. Broken glass crunched beneath his shoes as he carried her to the bedroom.

Claire didn't notice or care how clean and soft the bed was as Ethan laid her down. A seductive growl rumbled deep in his throat, and she helped him undress, forcefully, urgently. She whimpered as he clutched her to him, then roughly pushed her back on the mattress. His growl vibrated through his chest, tingling against Claire with the promise of lust, of abandon. Ethan was fighting against the transformation, as if wanting to - no, *needing* to - take her as a man, in human form.

Claire stifled an urge to howl, some distant part of her brain knowing that she was in a cottage in a village, not out in the forest beneath the moon. What if the neighbours heard? Called the police? What if Old Man Glover's hunt party-

She shuddered as Ethan's tongue grazed her thigh. She opened her legs wider and arched her back.

Ethan's tongue again . . . slowly licking across her . . .

She couldn't fight the change after that - couldn't fight who she was. What she was. What she wanted. Her true form undulated just beneath the surface of her human flesh. Claire almost laughed at the irony of even trying to resist the change. Ethan was going to prove to be oh-so-much-more than she imagined.

Her howl pierced the night as her skin began to stretch.

-XII-
Peeping Tom

It was enough to suffer the disparaging comments of his father, along with the humiliation of his sniggering cronies, but to see Claire kissing that chimp Ethan was more than Mark could bear.

He had snuck from the Jack and Jenny while his father gave his overblown speech, leaving the ridiculousness of the monster hunt to the simple minds of others. He had a hunt of a very different kind on his mind as he followed Claire out of the pub; but that was all forgotten now, and he still couldn't believe what he witnessed from the shadows. It had been a deep kiss, passionate, full of the kind of affection that Mark had sought from Claire himself. When the kiss had broken, and Ethan led Claire away by the hand, Mark knew exactly where they were headed. His blood boiled as he pursued them.

Cutting across the cornfields, he snuck up on the rear of the old cottage that had once belonged to Ethan's grandmother. He hopped over the low garden fence, and then headed across the lush, well-kept lawn towards the backdoor. Beyond it, the kitchen lights were on, but no one could be seen. The door was locked when he tried it, but Mark wasn't to be deterred; he wouldn't stand to be humiliated any further. He crept around the side of the house, his resolve hardening with bitter resentment.

Claire had lapped up his attention, accepted every penny he spent on her without complaint, even while she prattled about being an independent woman. Mark had played the courtship game, done more than enough to make her his, but not so much as a hand on his knee or the brush of her lips against his cheek in return. He had shown her more patience than she deserved, and this was how she dared repay him?

No, no, no – Claire would learn the hard way tonight that Glastonbury looked after its own, and she was no longer welcome among its townsfolk. As for Ethan . . . well, that imbecile could kiss his job goodbye as well as his American harlot-

Mark froze as a howl shattered the night's stillness. It was long, high-pitched, almost like human screaming. He looked behind him, half expecting his father's monster to be following him down the side of the cottage. But as the howl cut off, he realised it had held a muffled quality, and hadn't come from outside at all. Whatever had created such a din was within Ethan's home.

His heart hammering, Mark crept forward. Just up ahead, light spilled from a window. He braved a look through it, into Ethan's bedroom . . . and clamped a hand of his mouth to prevent the cry escaping his lips.

Ethan was naked, thrashing around on the bed as he fought some kind of mad dog, a wild beast . . . a *wolf*! But no – he wasn't fighting with it, Mark realised; he was . . . he was . . .

Kneeling behind the wolf, Ethan arched his back, opened his mouth impossibly wide, and shouted at the heavens. It was a long shout, drawn out, full of lust and violent pleasure, and it singed Mark's nerves. Was he calling Claire's name? Mark didn't get time to decide as the shout became another howl, and Ethan began to change.

His sweat-soaked skin rippled, shifted, and his body altered shape as bones elongated. Even through the glass of the window, Mark could hear the horrendous crackling sound as Ethan's skeleton reoriented itself into a very different form. Dark grey and bright silver hairs began to sprout from his back, his chest and stomach, arms and legs, head and face . . .

In an instant, it seemed, a second wolf was on the bed.

"Werewolf," Mark whimpered, and he pissed himself.

With a snarling of pleasure and pain, a clashing of sharp teeth, the wolves knocked a bedside lamp to the floor. The room was stepped in sudden darkness, and the beasts became dull, glowing blurs as they continued to thrash around.

Mark wanted to flee. He wanted to find his father, tell him he was sorry, that he believed all the old stories now, and then bring the townsfolk and their shotguns to this old cottage that had once belonged to Ethan's grandmother. But he was rooted to the spot.

He flinched as a face thumped against the window, and luminous yellow eyes glared at him through the glass. Mark stared back at the wolf for a fleeting moment, long enough to know they were Ethan's eyes looking at him. And then he ran, down the side of the house, across the well-kept lawn, and fell over the fence into the cornfield beyond.

As he got to his feet and fled, the sound of shattering glass followed him, and Mark screamed.

"Monsters!"

-XIII-
The Hunt

With his glowing pelt bejewelled with broken glass, Ethan chased after Mark.

He vaulted the garden fence smoothly, and he could hear Claire panting behind him. There was no need for communication now, no planning or plotting required; they knew what had to be done as soon as they ran into the cornfield. Claire darted away to the left, and Mark headed right. The hunt was on.

Silent and fast, like the sharpest scythe, Ethan cut through the tall stalks of corn, following the weak and desperate sound of Mark's wailing. He felt a thrill of pride and desire as he imagined Claire's sleek form doing the same on the other side of the field. With a surge of strength, he increased his speed. It didn't take long to overtake his prey, and block its path.

Mark almost ran into Ethan, spying him at the last moment as he entered a clearing of barren ground in the field, and skidding to a halt in the dry dirt. With his hackles raised, Ethan fixed him with a fierce stare, and bared his teeth as a growl rumbled in his throat.

Mark held out shaking hands in a placating gesture, choking on his words as he half pleaded, half sobbed, for mercy.

"Please-please don't kill me . . ."

Ethan could smell that Mark had soiled himself, and to witness how truly pathetic the man was offended him. With a snort, he took a step forward. Mark tried to skip back, but tripped and fell on his rump. A puff of dust rose and twinkled in the moonlight. Ethan's prey began weeping with deep, wracking sobs. He groaned the word,

"No," and held his hands before his face as the wolf took another step forward: a desperate act that could in no way protect him.

However, Ethan didn't attack, didn't move in for the kill. Instead, he allowed a moment to pass as he loomed over his prey. The corn encircling the clearing sighed in the gentle breeze.

Mark's weeping quickly reduced to small and childlike hiccups, and he slowly lowered his hands. Every inch of his face was etched with fear.

"Ethan? Ethan, it's you, isn't it?" he said with trembling lips. "Let me live," he begged. "I-I won't tell a soul, I promise."

It was a hollow claim, of course: a small, pathetic lie to save a small, pathetic man. Had Ethan been in human form, he might have laughed. As it was, he cocked his head to one side and bared his teeth in an approximation of a grin. The corn to his right shook. Mark barely had time to register the movement before a sleek, luminous form burst into the clearing and crashed into him.

Claire clamped her teeth around Mark's throat as she bowled him over onto his back. She snarled and shook and ripped out his larynx with a dark spray of blood. Mark's scream was cut short, as were his weak struggles. Claire continued biting and ripping at the dead man's throat, and the scent that filled the air made Ethan giddy. Human blood: just the smell was intoxicating and made him yearn for the ecstasy of its alien taste - a taste that Claire now revelled in.

Ethan's loins stirred as she looked up, standing on Mark's corpse, her bright muzzle matted black as she howled at the round and silver moon.

He made to move forward, to join Claire in this last and greatest taboo, but the corn hissed as the wind pick up and brought a new scent to his nostrils. His sense of danger flared, and he barked a warning to Claire, and her howl died away instantly.

Ethan saw the barrel of the rifle poking through the corn before he saw then man holding it. The weapon was aimed at Claire. Ethan jumped between them an instant before the crack of the gun shattered the night air. The bullet tore through his side, and he crashed to the ground.

Strangely, there was little pain, but the strength fled from Ethan's body so fast, so completely, that he could feel the wolf flowing from him like water down a drain. He was vaguely aware of a shout of anguish and pain, coupled with snarls and the gnashing of angry teeth. By the time Claire loomed over him and licked his face, Ethan had reverted to human form.

He turned his head and looked to where the gunman lay slaughtered. His dead eyes stared at Ethan, and his blood-streaked face was instantly recognisable. Of all people, it was Bill Parcy.

The angry shouts of men came from the near distance, and they were getting closer. Old Man Glover's hunt party had found them and were getting closer.

Ethan managed to sit up, stifling a yell as pain flared in his side. Claire whined and nuzzled him to get to his feet, but he knew he wouldn't get far before the hunt caught up with him.

"Run," Ethan told her. "They'll kill you."

But Claire didn't move. Her yellow eyes somehow expressed she wouldn't leave him.

Ethan gripped her ears and pulled her forehead to his. Her breath was warm on his face. "Thank you," he said. "For everything. But I can't come with you."

She whined again.

"No. You know it's true. Now *run!*"

He pushed Claire away from him. She hovered close to the clearing's edge, staring at him as the sound of angry men grew closer.

"I'll find you. I promise. Please – *go!*"

Claire howled again as she bounded off into the field; this time the sound was full of loss and frustration.

Slowly, painfully, Ethan crawled across the ground until he was hidden amidst the corn. Lying down, he held a hand to the wound at his side, slick with blood, and took several deep breaths. From his position, he still had a slight view of the clearing through the bases of the stalks. He watched as a pair of feet ran into the clearing. He heard a man retching, followed by an oath sworn to God.

"Glover was right," the man called out. "It was that American bitch. She got Bill Parcy. Glover's son, too!"

He was answered by a shout not too far off. "I see her!" The roar of a gun blistered the night. "She's headed for the wood!"

The man in the clearing ran off to join his friends.

As the shouts of the hunt party faded to the distance, Ethan wondered if he should just lie where he was, or brave the pain and search for some kind of sanctuary.

Either way, he knew he was dying.

-XIV-
RUSTIC SILVER

In the old and rundown barn, Claire whined softly and scratched at the steps leading up to the hayloft, testing the strength of the dry wood with her front paws, and then began to climb. She paused to lick a middle rung. Blood. Ethan's blood. The taste of it did not return Claire to the wild ecstasy she had experienced tasting Mark's blood. She whined again, and stifled the howl of deep misery that threatened to tear from her throat, less it led the hunt party to this place. But she was frozen, too fearful to continue up the steps and see what would be waiting for her.

She knew Ethan was up there; she had tracked his scent, first giving Glover's men the slip in the wood, and then doubling back to this old barn. But would she find him alive or dead?

First tentatively, then with more determination, she clambered up the remaining steps to the loft, to her Ethan. Her love.

He lay naked upon the floorboards, beneath the moonlight that shone down through a hole in a roof. His eyes were open, and Claire saw they still held a soft, warm glow. As she crept towards him, he gave her a weak smile, and Claire's heart flipped.

She nuzzled his neck, savoured the sensation of her silvery pelt against his sweaty skin, his hot breath mingling with hers. She licked him clean of blood, the worst of it where the bullet had hit his side. When she drew her tongue away, the blood kept flowing.

He raised a hand and laid it gently upon the side of her face. "Silver bullet," he whispered. "It's too late for me,

Claire." He took a shuddery breath. "I'm glad you came back, but you have to leave town."

Claire whined and nuzzled him again, but Ethan's hand thumped to the floorboards as he fell unconscious. His breathing became shallow.

Claire sat down heavily. She knew what he said was true; from the moment she saw the wound, she knew that Ethan would die. But the change from denial to acceptance was so hard and fierce, it sapped Claire's strength and she began to revert to human form. When the heat in her blood had cooled, when the ache and pain in her bones had dulled, she sat in the loft, coated with sweat, sobbing deeply.

She fell across Ethan's chest. "You can't die," she wept. "Not now. You can't be the last of your line. You-you-"

Claire's head snapped up as she heard a sound.

The barn doors had opened. Someone was shuffling across the dusty floor below.

Panic rose in her chest. She was naked, defenceless and too weak to change back into the wolf, to fight and protect her and Ethan. All she could do was wait hopelessly, breath held, heart thumping, as someone climbed the stairs . . .

To Claire's surprise, a well-stuffed rucksack was thrown into the hayloft. And this was quickly followed by a face appearing over the last rung - a fierce visage with eyes that could cut stone and pierce the soul.

"Doris?" Claire whispered.

The elderly landlady of the Jack and Jenny pub groaned with the effort of climbing the final few steps. She picked up the rucksack, and her expression softened with a sad smile as she held it out to Claire.

"Some clothes for you," she said.

Claire was vaguely aware of accepting the rucksack, but continued to stare at the old woman in disbelief.

"Don't gawp – dress!" Doris said as she knelt down on

cracking knees beside Ethan. "A lady should always keep her modesty, whatever the situation."

Speechless, Claire opened the rucksack and found a pair of jeans and a T-Shirt, a couple pairs of flip-flops, and a thin dress of floral design, which she pulled on. It was an old-fashioned number, a little too big for Claire's frame, but it covered her *modesty* well enough.

As Claire slipped on the flip-flops, Doris said, "That dress belonged to Mabel - Ethan's grandmother. I stopped by the cottage to pick you up a few things." Her eyes had lost their sharpness. "You did well to give Glover's men the slip, but it wasn't enough. I told them I saw you going off towards the Tor. They're on the other side of town now, so you have a little time yet."

"Thank you," Claire said, and fresh tears came to her eyes. "But it's too late. Ethan's been shot, and-"

"Hush up," Doris said, and returned her attentions to Ethan.

Hanging from her shoulder was a small leather pouch. She opened it and pulled out a little bottle containing a liquid that glowed faintly when she shook it.

"I never did know what this stuff's made from," Doris said. "Mabel used to call it Moonlight, and the recipe died with her. But I do know it's a cure for silver poisoning. She kept it in case of emergencies. Like now."

Claire's stomach flipped. "Then . . . he'll live?"

In answer, Doris popped the cork on the little bottle, and then poured a small amount of the glowing liquid onto Ethan's wound. He groaned but didn't wake as the Moonlight fizzed and bubbled and stopped the flow of blood.

"Give me a hand," Doris said.

Without hesitation, Claire moved forward and helped to roll Ethan onto his side. The elderly landlady applied more Moonlight to the wound where the bullet had exited on his back. With both wounds clean and no longer bleeding, Doris took a roll of gauze from the leather pouch, and Claire held Ethan in a sitting position while she wrapped his body.

"Strange, the people you meet in life," Doris said distantly as she wrapped. "No telling who's coming your way."

Claire frowned, but didn't say anything as she continued.

"Ethan's mum was a nice girl. Lucy was her name – quiet, kind, wouldn't hurt a fly, you know? But when she met Ethan's dad, I knew she'd met a wrong'un. So did Mabel. Not a lot you can do, though, when love's involved."

"You knew Ethan's father?" Claire asked.

"Vaguely." Doris sighed. "From out of town, he was – a loner or drifter, I suppose you Yanks would call him. But me and Mabel knew exactly what he was. Unfortunately, so did Old Man Glover."

Claire's mouth hung open. "It was him," she whispered. "All those years ago, it was Ethan's father they killed."

Doris's silence affirmed the answer. "After Lucy died in childbirth, Mabel brought Ethan up by herself, and she knew he bore his father's curse. But when she got ill . . ." She looked as though she was fighting sudden tears, but when she spoke again, her voice had steel in it. "Well – let's just say I promised Mabel I'd keep an eye on Ethan, and that's exactly what I've been doing the past ten years."

Claire remained silent as Doris finished wrapping Ethan's body, and they laid him back down on the bare boards. With a gnarled but steady hand, Doris poured the remaining Moonlight into Ethan's mouth. He spluttered a little as he swallowed, but still he didn't regain consciousness.

"There," Doris said. "Give him a little while and he should be right enough to walk. Then both of you can leave. Can't stay here now. You can cut across the field to the next town easy enough."

Claire didn't know what to say, could think of no way to express her gratitude to this stern and wiry old woman who had brought hope to hopelessness. To say, "Thank you," again was all she could think of.

The sharp edge came back to Doris's eyes. An instant later, her dry hand flashed out and slapped Claire hard across the face.

Claire reeled back and held her stinging cheek.

"You killed men tonight," Doris accused furiously. "Bill Parcy, I can understand – he had a gun and you defended yourself. But Mark Glover . . .?

"He saw us," Claire replied, angrily. "He would've told someone-"

"Don't give me that!" Doris retorted. "You didn't have to kill him. You could've packed your bags and pissed off." She shook her head, bitterly. "You should've listened when Old Man Glover was talking. He might be an ignorant bastard, but he was on to you from the beginning. He told the truth when he said he wouldn't follow you if you left town. Glastonbury business stays in Glastonbury."

"I didn't know," Claire said. "I-I wouldn't-"

"Deed's done now." Doris's voice was low and menacing. "I've already seen what outliving a daughter did to Mabel. God knows what losing his son will do to Glover."

With that, she rose on creaking knees and headed back toward the steps. She stopped, inhaling and exhaling heavily as she turned back.

"Here," she said, throwing the leather pouch to Claire. "It's the last of the Moonlight. I'd use it wisely, if I were you."

Bewildered, scared, Claire clutched the pouch and watched as the elderly landlady began to descend the steps. Just before her head disappeared, she blurted, "It was me."

Doris paused on the steps and glared at her.

"Ethan," Claire explained. "He didn't kill anyone."

"Ah, but he would've, given half the chance," Doris said with bitter disappointment. "That boy has lived his life keeping himself to himself – a danger to no one, just like his mother. But then *you* come along - a wrong'un - and . . ."

The elderly landlady struggled to regain her composure, and genuine, deep remorse came to her craggy face. "It a noble thing to continue a family's bloodline," she said, and her voice had softened again. "I truly hope Ethan gives you the babies you're craving. But when those mites grow old enough, I want you to tell them the story of tonight. And tell them the truth. Tell them how wrong you were. Because . . ."

She licked her lips and gritted her teeth. "Because if *they* start hunting people instead of cattle, then I hope a silver bullet finds the lot of you. Now get out of my town!"

And Doris disappeared, creaking down the steps, shuffling across the dusty floor, and the barn doors shuddered closed behind her.

Claire stared into empty space for a moment, but then a groan escaped Ethan's throat.

"Hey," Claire soothed as his eyes fluttered open. "How're you feeling?"

He thought about it for a second. "Not bad," he whispered in surprise, and then smacked his lips. "Bad taste in my mouth, though."

"You and me both," Claire replied, and her tears splashed onto his chest.

Ethan raised a hand to her face. "Claire, I should be dead."

Claire sobbed a laugh and held up the little leather pouch. "You have a guardian angel, Ethan."

He gave her a questioning look.

"Later," Claire said. "Come on. Let's get out of town."

About the authors . . .

Edward Cox lives in England with his wife and daughter. His first novel, The Relic Guild, was published in 2014 and he has been on a roll since. When not writing, he cheers for the West Ham FC [Up Irons!] and pines for the bacon and bear claws to which he was introduced during a visit to the Colonies in 2011. He is a graduate of Luton University, which some say was the inspiration for this novella.

Terrie Leigh Relf lives in San Diego and works as a Life Coach and Reiki Master. She has taught English, and Creative Writing, and is the author of a how-to book for speculative poetry [The Poet's Workshop and Beyond]. She likes Ethiopian coffee, moong daal, and of course chocolate. She edits the periodic drabble contest for Hiraeth Publishing.

www.ingramcontent.com/pod-product-compliance
Lightning Source LLC
LaVergne TN
LVHW021304080526
838199LV00090B/6008